The Firekeeper's Son

The Firekeeper's Son

by LINDA SUE PARK

Illustrated by JULIE DOWNING

sandpiper

Houghton Mifflin Harcourt
Boston New York

The illustrations were executed in watercolor and pastel.
The text was set in 16-point Tiepolo Bold.

All rights reserved. Published in the United States by Sandpiper, an imprint of Houghton Mifflin Harcourt
Publishing Company, Boston, Massachusetts. Originally published in hardcover in the United States by
Clarion, an imprint of Houghton Mifflin Harcourt Publishing Company, New York, 2004.

SANDPIPER and the SANDPIPER logo are trademarks of Houghton Mifflin Harcourt Publishing Company.

For information about permission to reproduce selections from this book, write to Permissions,
Houghton Mifflin Harcourt Company, 215 Park Avenue South, New York, New York 10003.

www.sandpiperbooks.com

Library of Congress Cataloging-in-Publication Data
Park, Linda Sue.
The firekeeper's son / by Linda Sue Park ; illustrated by Julie Downing.
p. cm.
Summary: In early-19th-century Korea, after Sang-hee's father injures his ankle,
Sang-hee attempts to take over the task of lighting the evening fire,
which signals to the palace that all is well. Includes historical notes.
HC ISBN-13: 978-0-618-13337-6
PA ISBN-13: 978-0-547-23769-5
[1. Signals and signaling—Fiction. 2. Fire—Fiction.
3. Korea—History—19th century—Fiction.]
I. Downing, Julie, ill. II. Title.
PZ7.P22115 Fi 2004
[E]—dc21   2002013917

Printed in China
SCP 10 9 8
4500561409

To Julie, sister and friend
—L. S. P.

To Ashley, Dwight, Martha, Mira, and Susan,
my guides in art and life
—J. D.

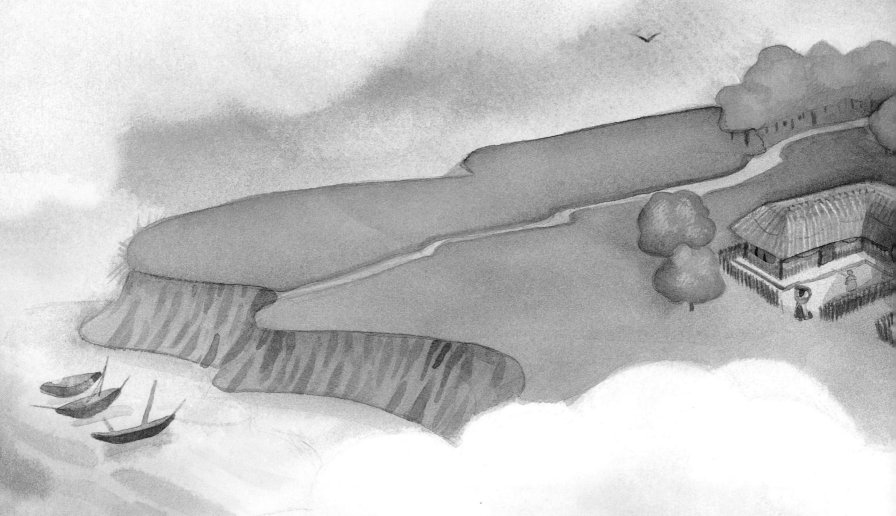

"We live in an important village," Sang-hee's father said.

Sang-hee looked around.
A few huts made of wood and mud.
A few cows.
A few chickens, a few dogs.
It did not look like an important village.

"Our part of Korea is like a dragon with many humps," his father said. "The humps are the mountains—the first hump facing the sea, the last hump facing the king's palace.

"Our mountain is the first hump.

"Our fire is the first fire."

9

Every evening at sunset Sang-hee's father climbed to the top of the mountain carrying a pair of tongs and a little brass pot filled with live coals.

Coals to start a fire.

A fire so big it could be seen from the next mountain.

Where another firekeeper saw it and lit *his* fire. A fire big enough to be seen from the *next* mountain.

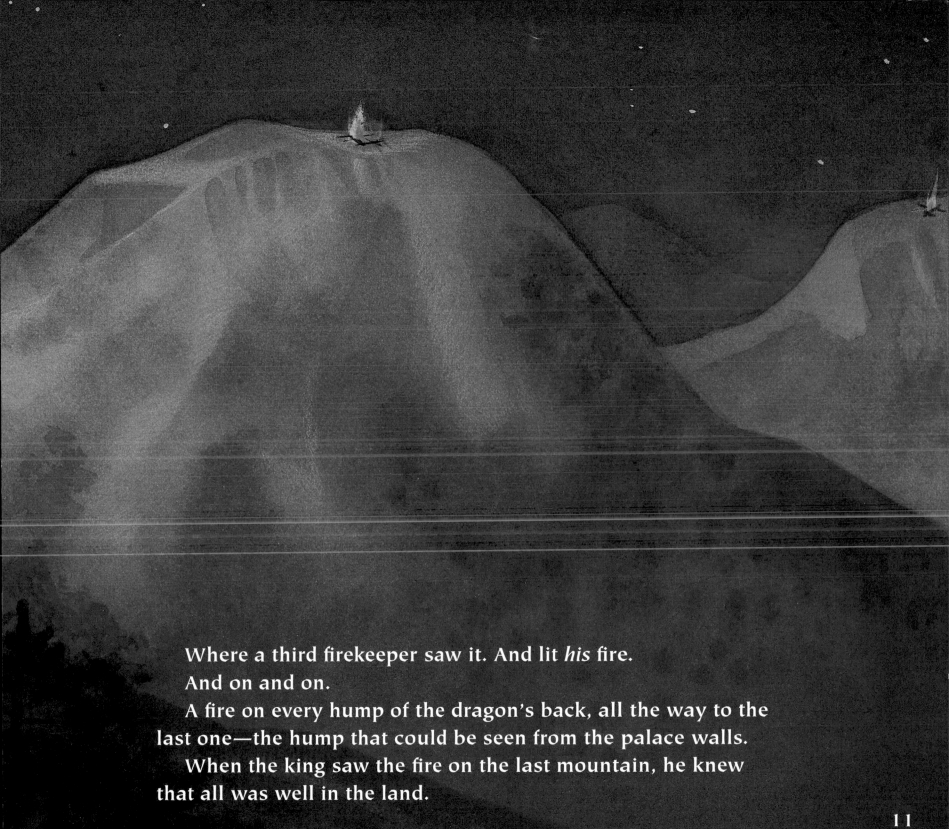

Where a third firekeeper saw it. And lit *his* fire.
And on and on.
A fire on every hump of the dragon's back, all the way to the
last one—the hump that could be seen from the palace walls.
When the king saw the fire on the last mountain, he knew
that all was well in the land.

"When trouble comes to our land, it almost always comes from the sea," Sang-hee's father explained. "If ever we see enemy ships, I will not light our fire. And the next firekeeper will not light *his* fire. And on and on, until the king sees only darkness on the last hump. He will know that trouble has come to our land, and he will send soldiers to fight the enemy.

"We are fortunate," Sang-hee's father said. "In your time, and my time, and your grandfather's time, the fire has always been lit.

"It is good to live in a time of peace.

"It is good that soldiers have never come."

Soldiers!
Tall, brave soldiers.
With shining swords.
Sang-hee wished he could see soldiers.
Just once.

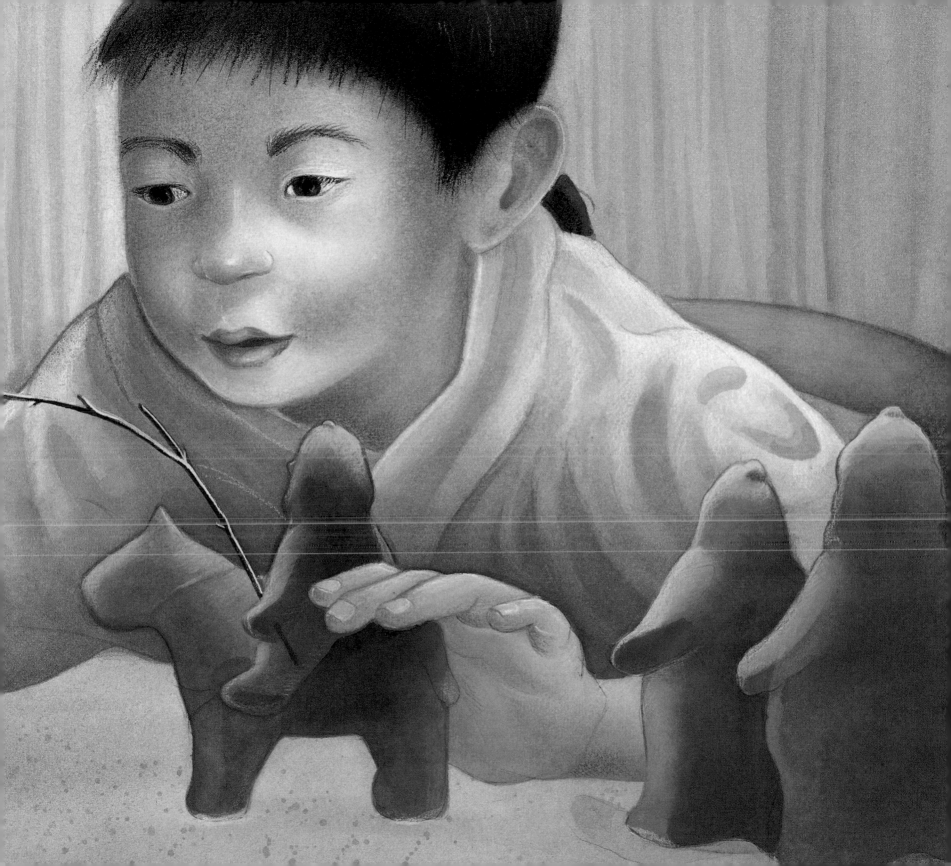

Evening.

Sang-hee shooed the chickens into their coop. He glanced up at the mountain, looking for the fire.

No fire. His father was a little late.

Sang-hee fetched water from the river. He poured the water into the barrel, then glanced up the mountain again.

No fire.

Sang-hee looked out at the sea, where the setting sun made a path on the water.

Could those be ships bobbing on the waves?

No. Just a flock of seagulls.

No enemies.

No trouble.

But still no fire.

18

Sang-hee called his mother. He pointed at the mountain.
She looked, then turned and stared at the sea. "Sang-hee,
you must run and see what has happened," she said.
"Something is wrong—there is no trouble from the sea,
and the fire must be lit!"

19

Sang-hee ran up the mountain path. He knew
the path like a friend.
But tonight it was not at all friendly.
Stones tripped him.
Branches reached out to lash at his face.
He ran until he could not run anymore.

A strange noise—a groaning sound.
A groan from the bushes by the path.
"Father!"
"Sang-hee, I am all right. But I fell and hurt my ankle, and I fear it is broken. I cannot walk. You must light the fire. Hurry!"

Sang-hee grabbed the brass pot and ran again.
The fire—he had to light the fire!
His feet pounded out a song on the path—*light the fire,*
light the fire, light the fire . . .

At last Sang-hee reached the top of the mountain.
There was the brush pile, ready to be lit. He knelt,
trembling from his run. He picked up one coal with
the tongs—and dropped it.

It broke into a hundred red jewels that glowed for
a moment, then died.

A second coal.

Gleaming bright as . . . as a soldier's sword.

If there is no fire, the soldiers will come. They will be angry when they find no enemies here.

But maybe—maybe not all of them will be angry.

Maybe there is a soldier who would be glad for a chance to visit the sea.

I could show him the beach.
Where to catch the best fish.
Where to find the prettiest shells.
After that he might teach me a little about sword-fighting . . .

27

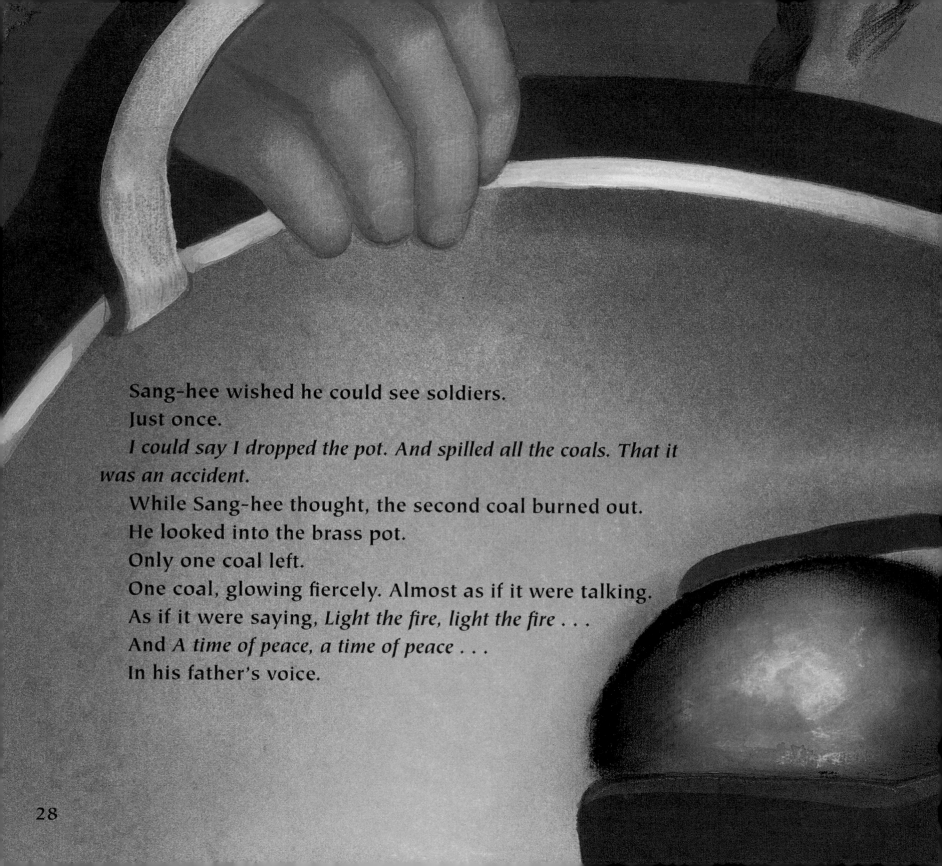

Sang-hee wished he could see soldiers.

Just once.

I could say I dropped the pot. And spilled all the coals. That it was an accident.

While Sang-hee thought, the second coal burned out.

He looked into the brass pot.

Only one coal left.

One coal, glowing fiercely. Almost as if it were talking.

As if it were saying, *Light the fire, light the fire . . .*

And *A time of peace, a time of peace . . .*

In his father's voice.

Sang-hee carefully picked up the last coal and put it on the tinder at the bottom of the brush pile. It smoked and smoldered, and for a moment it looked as if it would go out.

Then a tongue of flame licked the tinder. It ate all the tinder and reached greedily for the brush. Soon the whole pile was aflame.

Sang-hee watched the flames.
He saw a great battle—soldiers,
their shining swords clashing . . .

32

After the fire died out, Sang-hee waited until
the ashes cooled, then swept them aside. He
built a new pile of brush for the next night.
As his father had always done.
And his grandfather before him.
Then Sang-hee walked back down the path.

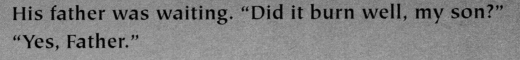

His father was waiting. "Did it burn well, my son?"

"Yes, Father."

He put an arm around his father's waist.

His father hobbled as they walked, and leaned on Sang-hee's shoulder. "When I was a boy, I too wished the soldiers would come."

Sang-hee drew in a quick breath. How did his father know?

"Do not forget, my son, that we are part of the king's guard just as the soldiers are. We are the very first part." Sang-hee's father smiled. "The village will be pleased to hear that another trustworthy firekeeper has been born to our family."

Suddenly, Sang-hee was glad he had lit the fire.

The gladness felt as warm as a glowing coal.

And until his father's ankle healed, it was Sang-hee who climbed the mountain every evening at sunset carrying the brass pot filled with live coals.

Coals to start a fire.

A fire that could be seen from the next mountain.

To tell another firekeeper to light *his* fire.

And on and on.

Until the king himself knew that all was well in the land.

Author's Note

Sang-hee and his family are fictional, but the bonfires were real. The bonfire signal system used in Korea was very complicated, and I have simplified it in the telling of this story, which is set in the early 1800s.

South Mountain—the last mountain facing the king's palace—actually had four bonfires. Each fire had two "halves"—the left and the right, as seen from the palace—and together the eight halves represented the country's eight provinces. Additional fires could be lit to convey further information, so the court would know not only which province was facing danger but things like the size of the enemy forces and how well armed they were!

My sources do not indicate when the lighting of the bonfires began. They were still being lit as recently as the late nineteenth century, when the practice was noted by Percival Lowell, an American astronomer and traveler, in his book *Choson: The Land of the Morning Calm,* published in 1885.

DATE D